Emily Just in Time

JAN SLEPIAN

ILLUSTRATED BY GLO COALSON

PHILOMEL BOOKS ◆ NEW YORK

Patricia Lee Gauch, editor.

Text copyright © 1998 by Jan Slepian. Illustrations copyright © 1998 by Glo Coalson.
All rights reserved. This book, or parts thereof, may not be reproduced in any form without
permission in writing from the publisher, Philomel Books, 200 Madison Avenue, New York, NY 10016.
Philomel Books, Reg. U.S. Pat. & Tm. Off. Published simultaneously in Canada.
Printed in Hong Kong by South China Printing Co. (1988) Ltd.
Book design by Gunta Alexander. The text is set in Breughel.
Library of Congress Cataloging-in-Publication Data
Slepian, Jan. Emily just in time/Jan Slepian; illustrated by Glo Coalson. p. cm.
Summary: As a small girl grows from "not-being-able, to now-she-can," she wonders if she
will ever spend a whole night at her grandmother's house without being afraid.
[1. Fear—Fiction. 2. Growth—Fiction. 3. Grandmothers—Fiction.] I. Coalson, Glo, ill. II. Title.
PZ7.S6318Em 1998 [E]—dc20 95-50002 CIP AC ISBN 0-399-23043-2 (hardcover)
10 9 8 7 6 5 4 3 2 1 First Impression

To Emily Bergen and her
Grandma, Jane—J. S.

To Deb Lewin and Helen Davies
for their courage and inspiration—G. C.

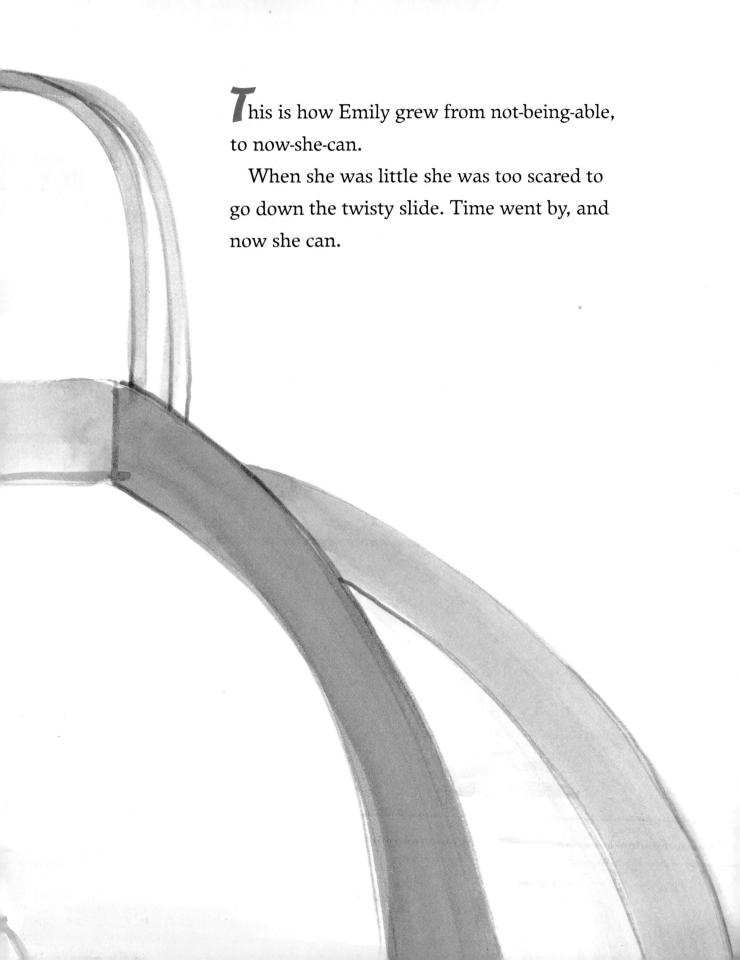

This is how Emily grew from not-being-able, to now-she-can.

When she was little she was too scared to go down the twisty slide. Time went by, and now she can.

When she was little she couldn't pour the milk on her cereal without spilling. Time passed, and now she can.

She couldn't do a cartwheel when she was little.
But in time she grew, and now she can.

What she can't do yet is stay the whole night through at her grandma's house.

Grandma's house is where she plays on rainy afternoons. Her favorite rocker is in the extra room. On the table next to the bed is her own mother's picture as a little girl. The night-light is a friendly clown. She loves to be with her grandma and wants to stay overnight.

But when she is tucked in the extra bed and Grandma kisses her goodnight, this is what happens.

Her eyes spring open. This isn't her room. It isn't her bed.

There's a noise in the corner that she doesn't know.

Her stomach bumps and her swallow hurts and she has to sit up to make room in her mouth for the cry to get out.

"Grandma! Grandma! I want to go home."

Her grandma gets dressed to take her home in the car.
"It's all right, my honey," her grandma says. "It just takes
time. Someday you'll stay the night and think nothing of it."

The next time she visits, Emily brings her own blanket from her bed. It smells like home and she nestles down with it under her cheek. Oh, yes. She is floating away in a cotton dream.

Then her eyes spring open and this isn't her bed, and what's that noise, and *bump* goes her stomach, she has to sit up to make room to cry, "Grandma! Grandma! I want to go home!"

Her grandma takes her home in the car and tells her again that it's all right. "A someday will come when you will stay the night. All it takes is time."

The next time she visits, Emily brings her bears and sits them on her pillow. Her bears will see her safely through the night. But when her eyes spring open, they know this isn't their bed. This isn't their room.

They all hear noises that they don't know. They tell her, "Sit up, make room. Cry out for your grandma. Get us home!"

Her grandma helps pack up the bears. She dries Emily's tears and says once more, "I promise the time will come. I promise that someday you'll stay the night and not think anything of it."

Then time goes by, and Emily goes on growing from not-being-able, to now-she-can. She once wasn't able to put her face in the water, and now she can.

She once wasn't able to color inside the lines.
But time went by, and now she can.

The limb of the tree, once too high for a jump,
she can suddenly reach with her fingertips.

Then comes a night in her grandma's house when she jumps on the bed in the extra room. Her blanket is home and so are her bears. She snuggles down to a cotton dream.

It isn't her bed, and it isn't her room, but she hears no noise in the corner. Nothing bumps.

Not once do her eyes spring open.

She has reached the someday when she can stay the night.

And Emily doesn't think anything of it.